BRADFORD STREET BUDDIES
Backyard Camp-Out

For Shannon Milam, with thanks for bringing the sticks —J.N.
For Gisela and John, I love you to pieces —M.H.

Text copyright © 2015 by Jerdine Nolen
Illustrations copyright © 2015 by Michelle Henninger

www.hmhco.com

The text of this book is set in Chaparral Pro.
The display type was set in Candy Round and Marujo.
The illustrations are drawn in ink and watercolor on Arches watercolor paper.

Library of Congress Cataloging-in-Publication Data
Nolen, Jerdine.
Backyard camp-out / by Jerdine Nolen.
p. cm. — (The Bradford Street buddies ; book 2) (Green light readers Level 3)
Summary: While preparing for a backyard campout, Jada and Jamal Perkins
join their friends Josh Cornish and Carlita Garcia in a search for Mrs. Mason's
lost cat, Daisy.
ISBN 978-0-544-36844-6 paperback
ISBN 978-0-544-36843-9 paper over board
[1. Friendship—Fiction. 2. Camping—Fiction. 3. Lost and found possessions—
Fiction. 4. Cats—Fiction. 5. Family life—Fiction. 6. African Americans—Fiction.]
I. Title.
PZ7.N723Bac 2015
[E]—dc23
2014006757

Manufactured in China
SCP 10 9 8 7 6 5 4 3 2 1
4500529171

BRADFORD STREET BUDDIES
Backyard Camp-Out

WRITTEN BY **JERDINE NOLEN**

ILLUSTRATED BY **MICHELLE HENNINGER**

Green Light Readers
HOUGHTON MIFFLIN HARCOURT
Boston New York

CONTENTS

1. Something Found

The Perkins family was cleaning out their garage.
"Look at this!" Jada called out to her twin brother, Jamal.
It was a big, bulky, clunky bag.
Metal parts were sticking out.

Jada and Jamal tried to move it, but it was too heavy.
"What do you think it is?" Jamal asked.

"It looks like you found the old tent," shouted
Mr. Perkins with a smile. "I had forgotten all about it."
"We had lots of fun camping out before you two were
born," Mrs. Perkins laughed.

Jamal and Jada looked at each other and shrugged. They could not imagine their parents camping.

"Does the tent still work?" Jamal asked.

"Probably," said Mr. Perkins.

"Let's put it up in the backyard," Jada suggested. "We could camp out under the stars!"

"That would be awesome!" Jamal agreed.

"Can we put it up?" asked Jada.

"PLEASE?" Jamal begged.

"Please, please, please?" they both pleaded together.

Mr. Perkins looked at Mrs. Perkins.

They both laughed.

"Camping out would be fun," said Mr. Perkins.

Muzzy barked. Jada and Jamal clapped.

"But we have to finish cleaning the garage first,"
Mrs. Perkins reminded them. "Let's keep going!"
She blew her handy whistle.
Everyone got back to work.

The kids whispered as they worked.
But they could not keep a secret very long.
"Can I invite Josh to the camp-out?" blurted out
Jamal.
"And Carlita," chimed in Jada.
Mr. and Mrs. Perkins smiled.
It was settled. Their best friends could come.

2. Something Lost

Mr. and Mrs. Perkins set up the tent.

Jada and Jamal helped.

"It looks great!" Jada said, running in and out of the tent. "Look—Muzzy wants to go camping too!"

"Let's go find Josh and Carlita," Jamal said.

But Carlita and Josh were already racing toward the Perkinses' yard.

Carlita was waving a sheet of paper over her head.

"Jada," Carlita called, almost out of breath.

"Jamal," Josh yelled. "Take a look at this!"

The paper had writing on the front.
It read:

"Oh, no," Jada said, picking up Muzzy and giving
him a hug. "Where can Daisy be?"

"That's what we're trying to find out," Josh said.
"Want to help us look for her?"

"Sure—let's go," Jamal said, looking at his parents.

"Mrs. Mason must be *very* worried," Mrs. Perkins said.

"If we work together I know we can find her," Carlita said.

"Hey!" Josh pointed. "What are you doing with the tent?"

"We were just coming to find the two of you," answered Jamal. "We want to invite you to our camp-out under the stars."

Jada smiled at Carlita. "Do you think you can come?"

"I never slept in at tent before," said Carlita.
"Camping sounds like fun, but let's find Daisy first."
Josh agreed.

"I'll call to make sure it's okay with your parents,"
Mrs. Perkins said. "We'll have a cookout too."
The kids went running.

3. Still Missing

It was suppertime. Jamal, Jada, Josh, and Carlita headed for the Perkinses' backyard.

"Any luck?" Mrs. Perkins asked.

"We looked for Daisy all over Bradford Street,"
Jamal said.

"We looked up into the trees," Jada said.

"We looked under porches," Carlita added.

"And we looked in the park,"
Josh said.

"Daisy has got to be around here somewhere,"
Jamal said. "She wouldn't just leave Mrs. Mason."

"I'm sorry you didn't find her," said Mr. Perkins.
"Soon it will be too dark to look, but I'm sure Daisy
will be all right."
"Sometimes pets like to hide," added Mrs. Perkins.

Mrs. Garcia and Mr. Cornell came into the yard.
Mrs. Garcia brought chocolate bars, graham crackers,
and marshmallows. Mr. Cornell had his guitar.
Mr. Perkins waved and whistled while he cooked
hamburgers on the grill.

"Hello, neighbors!" said Mrs. Perkins.
"The food will be ready in a few minutes.
Make yourselves comfortable!"

Everyone was enjoying the cookout.

Suddenly Mrs. Garcia thought about something.

"Carlita, did you remember to feed Henry and put
him in his crate?" Mrs. Garcia asked.

"Yes, Mom. Don't worry—Henry won't get lost."

Jada and Carlita were laying out their sleeping bags.
"I can't wait to make s'mores," Carlita said.

Josh smiled. "Mmm, camping is going to taste
delicious," he said.

Jamal and Josh were checking the flashlights and batteries.

"Do we have enough batteries?" Carlita asked.

"We can do more searching for Daisy around the backyard," Jada said.

"I hope we find her soon." Carlita sighed.

4. A Great Find

"It's almost time to toast marshmallows,"
Mrs. Garcia called.
"We need sticks," Josh said. Everyone grabbed a
flashlight and headed for the woodsy area at the
edge of the yard.

CRUNCH! CRUNCH! CRUNCH!

"Did you hear that?" Jamal asked.

"It was just the wind rustling some leaves,"
Carlita said.

"But the wind isn't blowing," Josh said.

CRUNCH! CRUNCH CRUNCH!

"There it is again!" said Jamal.

"Maybe it was a cricket," Jada said.

"That didn't sound like a cricket to me," Jamal said.

Something was moving around in the bushes.

SCRUNCH, SCRUNCH, SCRUNCH!
CRUNCH, CRUNCH, CRUNCH!

Carlita whispered, "I heard it that time. What is it?"

"Maybe it's Daisy," Jada said.

"There's only one way to find out," Josh said.

"On the count of three, shine your light on the
bushes," Jamal said.
"One, two, three!"

"What *is* that?" Jada asked.

Two bright eyes shone back at them.

"Henry!" Carlita screamed. "How did you get out of your crate?"

Henry was standing by the tree with the hole in it.

"Come here, boy."

But Henry did not move.

Jada looked again. "Hey, there's Muzzy, too.
Muzzy, what are you doing over there?
Come over here, Muzzy," Jada said.
But Muzzy would not move either.

"Did you hear that?" Jamal asked.
"Listen *very* carefully."

Meow, meow, meow, they heard over and over again.
The sounds came from the hole in the tree.

"Shine your light there, Jamal—you're tallest,"
Josh said.
Two yellow eyes reflected back. *Meow.*

"It's Daisy!" Carlita screamed.

"Not just Daisy," Jamal said. "It's Daisy and four kittens."

"KITTENS! Daisy had kittens?" Jada yelled.

Jada and Carlita jumped up and down.

"I'd better go get Mom and Dad," Jada said.
"Everybody will want to see them."

"I'll keep the flashlight on the kittens," Jamal said.
"I'll stay with Muzzy and Henry," Carlita said.
"I'll go get Mrs. Mason," Josh said. "She will be so surprised to find out that Daisy had kittens."

"She will be so happy to know that Daisy is safe,"
Jamal said.

"Yes," Carlita said.

"Muzzy and Henry made sure of that!"